Firehouse Fun!

by ABBY KLEIN

illustrated by
JOHN McKINLEY

Scholastic Inc.
New York Toronto London Auckland Sydney
Mexico City New Delhi Hong Kong Buenos Aires

This book is dedicated to Captain Ken
and the South Burlington Fire Department,
who keep the citizens of South Burlington
safe every day.
—A. K.

ISBN-13: 978-0-545-13042-4
ISBN-10: 0-545-13042-5

12 11 10 9 8 7 6 5 4 3 2 1   9 10 11 12 13 14/0

Printed in the U.S.A.
First printing, September 2009

CHAPTERS

I have a problem.

A really, really, big problem.

My class is going on a field trip
to the fire station. At the end of
the visit, the captain is going to
choose three people to slide down
the fire pole. I'm afraid to slide
down that pole, but I don't want
anyone to know, because then
they will think I am a baby.

Let me tell you about it.

CHAPTER 1

Field Trip Surprise

"Boys and girls," said my teacher, Mrs. Wushy, "please come and sit on the rug. I have a special surprise to tell you about."

"Cool," I said to my best friend, Robbie. "I love surprises."

"Me, too," Robbie said. "I can't wait to hear what it is!"

We all started to walk over to the rug except for Max. As usual, he was running and not watching where he was going. He bumped right into Chloe, and she went flying toward the carpet.

"Wah, wah, wah!" she wailed as soon as she hit the floor.

Mrs. Wushy came running over. "Chloe, what happened?"

"M-M-M-Max pushed me down."

"I didn't push you, you little baby," Max said.

"Oh, yes . . . you . . . did," Chloe sobbed.

"No, I didn't!"

"Yes, you did."

"All right. Enough, you two," said Mrs. Wushy. "I think Max accidentally bumped into you."

"Yeah. That's right. It was an accident," mumbled Max.

"Well, even if it was an accident, you still need to say you're sorry," said Mrs. Wushy.

"Sorry," Max mumbled.

"He didn't say it, Mrs. Wushy," Chloe whined.

"Sorry!" Max yelled in her face.

"Max, that was not very polite," said Mrs. Wushy. "Please do not yell in people's faces. I would like you to find a seat on the rug."

"But what about me?" Chloe sobbed.

"What about you?" asked Mrs. Wushy. "You can go sit on the rug, too."

"But what about my finger?" Chloe continued. "It's bleeding!" She held up her finger for all of us to see.

"I don't see any blood, do you?" my friend Jessie whispered in my ear.

"Nope. Nothing," I whispered back.

"That girl is such a drama queen," said Jessie.

"You can say that again," said Robbie. "I think she should be an actress when she grows up. She definitely knows how to put on a show!"

"Come with me, Chloe," said Mrs. Wushy. "We'll get you a Band-Aid."

Chloe went with Mrs. Wushy to get a Band-Aid for her invisible cut, and the rest of us sat down on the rug. Unfortunately, Max sat down right next to me.

"Hey, move over, Shark Boy," Max barked. "You're squishing me."

"More like *you're* squishing *me*," I said under my breath.

Max stuck his face right in mine. "What did you say?"

Oh great! Why didn't I just keep my big mouth shut? Now the biggest bully in the whole first grade looked like he was about to punch me.

As I was trying to figure out what to do next, Mrs. Wushy and Chloe came back to the rug. "Okay, everybody, now I think we can get started," Mrs. Wushy said.

Max turned around.

I sighed with relief. "Whew, that was a close one," I whispered to Robbie.

"It sure was," said Robbie, shaking his head. "It sure was."

"As I was saying," said Mrs. Wushy, "I have a surprise for all of you."

"A surprise! A surprise!" we all cheered. "Tell us what it is! Tell us what it is!"

"If everyone will please be quiet, then I can tell you."

All of a sudden the room got really quiet. Everyone stared at Mrs. Wushy, waiting to hear what she had to say.

"Well, as you all know, October is Fire Safety Month, so I thought it would be fun to go visit a real fire station."

"All right!" Max yelled, pumping his fist in the air. "I love fire stations. Are we going to go to the one right down the street?"

"As a matter of fact, we are," said Mrs. Wushy. "You all know Ms. Sue, who works in the office, right?"

We all nodded.

"Well, her husband is the captain of that fire station, and he has invited us to visit the station and take a very special tour."

"I'm going to slide down the fire pole," Max said excitedly.

All of a sudden I got a knot in my stomach.

"Oh, I don't think you'll be allowed to do that," Mrs. Wushy said, smiling.

The knot went away.

"Yes, you can," said Max. "I went to visit the fire station in preschool, and at the end of the tour, the firefighter picked three kids to slide down the fire pole."

"That sounds like so much fun!" said Jessie. "I want to do it!"

Chloe wrapped her arms around herself. "Oooooh, I'm scared!" she said, pretending to shiver. "I don't want to do it."

"You're such a baby," said Max.

"Is it the real pole that the firefighters slide down?" asked Robbie.

"Yep. I think it's like two stories high," Max said, jumping up to stand on a chair. "Much higher than this," he said, stretching his arm above his head.

"Max, get down off that chair right away," said Mrs. Wushy. "We never stand on chairs. That is very dangerous!"

Max jumped down.

"Well, we'll see," said Mrs. Wushy. "I'm sure if that's true, then the captain is going to pick the kids who have been the best listeners and been on their very best behavior."

"I know I'm going to get picked," said Max.

"Yeah, right," Jessie whispered to me. "But I bet you'll get picked, Freddy. Won't that be great?"

"Yeah. Great," I said weakly, trying to smile.

"The trip is tomorrow," said Mrs. Wushy, "so please bring this permission slip back to me in the morning, or else you won't be able to go."

Maybe I could lose that slip on the way home or be lucky enough to come down with the flu by the next morning. After all, my stomach was already in so many knots, I thought I was going to throw up. I really didn't want to slide down that pole. It was way too high up, and I was afraid of being that far off the ground. But if I didn't do it, then Max would call me a baby just like Chloe. I didn't know what was worse: sliding down the pole or having everyone think I was a fraidy-cat. I was going to need some help, and I was going to need it fast!

CHAPTER 2

Help!

After school that day, Robbie came over to my house to play. When we got off the bus, my mom was waiting for us.

"Hi, boys. Come on in. I made you a special snack."

As soon as we walked inside, I knew what it was, because the sweet, chocolaty smell filled the house. I took a long sniff. "Mmmmmmmm, I think that is my favorite smell in the whole world."

"It smells really good in here, Mrs. Thresher," said Robbie.

"Thank you. Would you boys like some warm brownies and milk?"

We threw our backpacks down and ran over to the kitchen table.

"Not so fast, boys. You need to go to the bathroom and wash your hands first," said my mom.

As we darted off to the bathroom, she called after us, "And don't forget to use the soap!"

My mom was such a neat freak. She didn't fall for that old trick of just rinsing your hands off with water. She could tell from a mile away whether you had used soap.

Robbie and I washed our hands and got back to the table just as my mom was setting down the plate of brownies. I leaned over and stuck my face in the plate and took a long whiff.

"Freddy! What are you doing?" said my mom. "Please get your head out of the plate!"

"But it just smells so good," I said, lifting my head and smiling.

"I'm glad you like them so much, but I don't think Robbie wants your germs all over them."

"Yeah," said Robbie. "Why don't you just eat one instead of kissing it?"

We both laughed, and then I picked one up and started shoving it into my mouth.

"Whoa, whoa, whoa, Freddy. Slow down," my mom said. "Where's the fire?"

"Fire? What fire?" I asked as a few brownie crumbs tumbled out of my mouth.

"Oh my goodness," said my mom. "Freddy, where are your manners? Please don't talk with your mouth full."

I took a sip of milk to wash down the brownie. "Sorry, Mom. Is there a fire somewhere?"

"Oh no, honey," my mom said, laughing. "'Where's the fire?' is just an expression that means you're doing something really quickly, as if there is a fire and you have to get out fast."

"Oh, I get it," I said, reaching for another brownie.

"Speaking of fires," said Robbie, "our class is going to visit the fire station tomorrow."

"Wow! That's exciting!" my mom said.

"I know," Robbie agreed. "And some lucky kids might get to slide down the fire pole."

"Maybe you'll be one of the lucky ones, Freddy," my mom said as she winked at me.

Oh yeah. Really lucky, I thought. Suddenly, I

didn't feel like eating anymore. I was starting to feel sick to my stomach. I stood up and grabbed Robbie by the arm. "Come on! We've got to go outside."

"But I'm not finished with my brownie yet."

"Then take it with you," I yelled as I yanked him out the door.

"What's your problem?" Robbie asked as soon as we got outside.

"If I tell you, do you promise not to tell anyone else?"

"I promise."

"You swear?"

"I swear. Scout's honor," Robbie said, holding up three fingers.

"I'm afraid of the fire pole," I whispered.

"You're afraid of the fire pole?" Robbie said loudly.

"Shhhhhhh!" I said, covering his mouth with my hand. "This is supposed to be a secret.

I really don't need the whole neighborhood to know."

Robbie nodded and gave me the "okay" sign with his fingers.

I took my hand off his mouth.

"Why are you afraid of the fire pole?"

"Do you remember the night we snuck outside to look for nocturnal animals, and I was swinging from a branch way up in the tree, and I fell and broke my arm?"

"How could I forget?" said Robbie.

"Well, ever since then, I've been afraid of being up high."

"Oh, so that's why you never want to climb the trees at the park, or go on the monkey bars at recess," Robbie said.

"The only problem is, nobody knows that's the reason, and I'd like to keep it that way. If Max knew the real reason, he'd never stop teasing me and calling me a baby."

"I get it now," said Robbie. "So what are you going to do tomorrow if you get picked?"

"I have no idea," I said, shaking my head and sighing a great big sigh.

"I have an idea," said Robbie.

"You do?"

"Yep. How about I be your coach, and we do some sliding practice?"

"I don't know. . . ."

"Come on, Freddy. Just try it."

"Well, okay," I muttered. "But I don't think it's going to work."

We walked over to the big tree in my yard. "Now," said Robbie, "just climb up a tiny bit, so you don't have to slide down very far. Watch me." Robbie climbed about two feet off the ground and then slid down the trunk of the tree. "Now you try it."

I climbed up about as far as Robbie had gone and then stopped.

"Come on, Freddy. You can do it!" said Robbie.

I took a deep breath and slid down. No problem.

"See! You can do it!" said Robbie. "Now this time just go a little higher."

I tried again. I climbed up the tree about three feet and slid right down.

"That was awesome, Freddy!" Robbie said, giving me a high five. "This time why don't you try climbing up as high as that branch?"

"But that's the branch I fell from," I said nervously.

"Just don't think about that. I know you can do it," said Robbie, patting me on the back. "Go for it!"

I took a deep breath and slowly climbed the tree until I was as high as the branch, and then I froze.

"Come on!" yelled Robbie. "You can do it!"

"No, I can't!" I yelled back.

"Yes, you can. Don't look down, and just slide."

My heart was beating so fast I thought it was going to pop out of my chest. I closed my eyes and started to slide, but when I was about halfway down, I lost my grip and fell to the ground with a thud.

Robbie came running over. "Freddy? Freddy? Are you all right?"

I lay on my back in the grass and looked up at Robbie. "Thanks for trying to help, but I'm doomed," I said. "I will never be able to slide down that fire pole, and everyone, including Max, will know what a fraidy-cat I am."

CHAPTER 3

Where's the Fire?

When my alarm went off the next morning, I jumped out of bed and started yelling, "Fire! Fire!"

My sister, Suzie, ran into my room. "What are you talking about, Shark Breath? There's no fire in here."

I blinked and looked around. "Oh, sorry," I said. "I was dreaming that I was a firefighter, and when my alarm went off, I thought it was the alarm in the fire station."

"Whatever, Weirdo," said Suzie. As she turned to walk out of the room, she said over her shoulder, "You know, your breath stinks. Your girlfriend Jessie won't want to kiss you if your breath smells like that!"

"First of all, she's not my girlfriend, and second of all, my breath doesn't stink. *You* stink!" I yelled after her.

I wish today was already over, I thought. *I really don't want to go on this field trip.* My thoughts were interrupted by my mom, who walked into my room.

"What's going on up here? I thought I heard some yelling."

"Nothing."

Just then Suzie barged in again, with her toothbrush hanging out of her mouth. "Freddy dreamt he was some big, brave firefighter," she said, laughing.

"Why are you laughing?" asked my mom.

"Because that's the funniest thing I've ever heard!"

"No, it's not," said my mom. "Freddy is very brave, and one day he might just grow up to be a firefighter. Right, Freddy?"

"Uh, yeah, right," I mumbled. Oh, if she only

knew! How could I ever be a firefighter if I was afraid to slide down the pole?

"Maybe in his dreams," said Suzie, accidentally spitting toothpaste out of her mouth.

"Suzie, you need to be nicer to your brother. Now please go back to the bathroom and finish brushing your teeth in there. I really don't want you spitting toothpaste on the rug."

"At least I brush my teeth," she said as she left the room.

"Now, Freddy," said my mom, "you've got to get a move on. You don't want to be late to school and miss the field trip."

Oh yes I do, I thought.

"Hurry up and get dressed and come downstairs for breakfast. I made you a special firefighter's breakfast. I want to see you in the kitchen in ten minutes."

After she left, I sat down on my bed and hit my forehead with the palm of my hand. "Think, think, think," I said to myself. "What am I going to do? I can't let anyone know that I'm afraid to slide down the fire pole."

"Did you say that you were afraid to slide down the fire pole?" Suzie asked, snickering.

Where had she come from? She should be a spy when she grows up. She knows how to sneak into a room without anyone noticing, and she has supersonic ears. She hears everything!

"Get out! Get out!" I yelled. "This is my room, and you're not allowed in here!"

"Okay, fine, little baby. I'm leaving. I'd better hurry up anyway, because I can't wait to get to school and tell my friends that you're afraid to slide down the pole."

I stared at her a minute. If she told people at school, then Max would tease me for the rest of my life! "You wouldn't do that."

"What's it worth to you?"

"Umm . . . umm."

"Let's go. I haven't got all day. The bus is coming soon."

"All right, all right, you can choose which computer games we play tonight."

"Tonight?" she said, snickering. "I get to choose for the next three nights, or no deal."

Three nights was way too long, but I really didn't have a choice. If she opened her big mouth at school, then my life was over. "Fine. The next three nights."

"Deal?" she said, holding up her pinkie for a pinkie swear. I held up mine, and we locked fingers.

"Deal," I said.

As she started to leave, I called after her, "Wait!"

"What? Did you change your mind?"

"No, I didn't change my mind. I was just wondering if you've seen my lucky shark's tooth. I have to have it for today, but it's not on my nightstand where I put it last night."

"It's in the bathroom."

"The bathroom? How'd it get in there?"

"I don't know. Maybe you left it in there when you got home from fighting fires last night."

"Very funny," I said.

I followed Suzie into the bathroom. "Here it is," she said, handing it to me.

"Thanks! You're the best sister in the whole world," I said, giving her a hug.

"I know," she said, smiling. "Now let go of me and brush your teeth. Your breath stinks. There's a reason I call you Shark Breath, you know."

CHAPTER 4

Doomed!

When we got to school, we put our backpacks away, and Mrs. Wushy told us all to line up.

"Line up?" said Chloe. "What for?"

"To go to lunch, Bubblehead," said Max.

"Lunch? But we just got here."

"Is she for real?" Robbie whispered to me.

"We're going to the fire station, Ding-Dong," said Max.

"But I just don't understand," Chloe whined.

"Why are we lining up now? I don't see a bus outside."

Just then Mrs. Wushy walked over. "We don't need a bus, Chloe."

"Why not?"

"Because we're walking."

"Walking? No one told me that! I can't walk that far in my brand-new pink satin ballet slippers."

"First of all," said Mrs. Wushy, "it's only three blocks. And second of all, I did write in the note to your parents that you should wear comfortable walking shoes."

"What am I going to do now?" Chloe whimpered.

"I have a suggestion," said Mrs. Wushy. "Do you have your sneakers for PE in your cubby?"

"Yes."

"Then why don't you put those on?"

"Those? But they're purple. They won't match my fluffy pink dress."

"Well, we're running out of time. We have to get to the fire station, so you can either put on your sneakers or miss the trip."

Chloe stuck out her lower lip in a big pout. "Fine. I'll put on the sneakers, but I'm going to look really silly."

"You look silly all the time," said Max.

"That's not nice, Max. You take that back," Chloe said, stamping her foot.

"All right, you two," said Mrs. Wushy. "You both need to stop. You're going to make us late. Max, leave her alone, and Chloe, go put on your sneakers."

After much fussing, Chloe finally got her sneakers on.

"I think we are all ready to go now," Mrs. Wushy said. "I am going to give everyone a buddy for the trip. When I tell you who your buddy is, please take each other's hands and line up."

"Not Max. Not Max," I whispered to myself. My day was bad enough already. I really didn't need it to get any worse.

Luckily, Mrs. Wushy made Robbie and me partners.

"High five, partner," Robbie said to me, giving me a high five.

Poor Jessie got stuck with Max. In a way that was good, because she was the only one in the class who was not afraid to stand up to him. I wish I could be as brave as her.

"Okay, grab your partner's hand and let's get going."

We walked out the school gate and down the block. "Remember, stay on the sidewalk," said Mrs. Wushy. "I don't want anyone too close to the street."

As we walked, Robbie and I started to talk. "So," said Robbie. "How are you feeling today, Freddy?"

"Oh, I don't know."

"Are you still too afraid to slide down the fire pole?" he whispered.

Just then our conversation was interrupted by Max. "Did I just hear you say that little baby Freddy is too afraid to slide down the fire pole?"

Great! Just great! I thought. *How did Max hear*

that? Now the whole class knows. But before I could say anything, Jessie said, "Of course Robbie didn't say that. Why would Robbie say that? Freddy would never be afraid to slide down the fire pole. Right, Freddy?"

"Uh, right," I said.

"In fact," said Jessie, "I bet Freddy can slide down quicker than you."

"Yeah, right," Max said, snickering. "I doubt it."

"We'll see," Jessie said, smiling.

We continued to walk down the street, and I could feel the knot in my stomach getting bigger and bigger as we got closer and closer to the fire station. "I'm doomed," I whispered to myself.

"What?" asked Robbie.

"Like I told you yesterday: I'm doomed."

"No, you're not," said Robbie. "You probably won't even be picked. So you should stop worrying about it."

"I just have this bad feeling that I will be

picked, and then I'll have to do it, because Jessie just told the whole class that I am not a fraidy-cat. I think I'm going to throw up."

Just then I heard Mrs. Wushy's voice from the front of the line. "Here we are at the fire station. Isn't it exciting? Let's go in and meet Captain Ken."

CHAPTER 5

Station 1

"Good morning, everyone," said Captain Ken.

"Good morning, Captain Ken," we all said.

"Welcome to fire station number one. Today I am going to give you a tour of the station, and then I have a special surprise for you at the end."

"I know! I know!" Max said, jumping up and down. "Some people get to slide down the fire pole."

"Uuuughhhh," I moaned quietly. Did he have to remind me?

"That's right," said Captain Ken. "How did you know?"

"Because I came here with my preschool."

"Excellent. Then you know a lot about our station, but for those of you who don't, you can ask me questions at any time during the tour, and I will be happy to answer them. Are you all ready to go?"

"Yes!" we all said excitedly.

"Well, let's start inside the firehouse, and then I will take you out into the garage to see the trucks. How does that sound?"

"Great!"

"Oh, I do want to remind you that at any time during the tour, the other firefighters and I may have to leave to respond to an emergency. I hope that doesn't happen, but if the alarm sounds, then we will have to jump in the trucks and take off."

"That would be cool to see," Robbie said to me.

"Yeah, and if he had to leave, then no one would have to slide down the pole," I said.

Robbie patted me on the back. "Stop worrying, Freddy. You'll be fine. I promise."

Captain Ken led us up to the second floor of the firehouse.

"Now, boys and girls," said Captain Ken, "when we are on duty, our shift is twenty-four hours long."

"That's a whole day, including the night!" said Chloe.

"That's right. That's why we have to have bedrooms up here in the fire station. The firefighters all have cots to sleep on and cubbies for their stuff."

"What's in the cubby?" asked Max.

"That's the firefighter's uniform. If the alarm goes off in the middle of the night, then the firefighters don't want to go all the way downstairs to put on their uniforms. That would waste time, so they keep their uniforms up here, and when the alarm sounds, they jump out of bed, throw on their uniforms, and slide down this big pole right here."

The pole! There it was . . . shiny and silver and really high up! My stomach started doing flips.

"Are you okay?" Robbie whispered.

"I think I'm going to be sick."

"Let's go visit the next room," said Captain Ken.

Yes, let's, I thought. *The farther away I am from that pole, the better.* We walked back downstairs.

"Now, I bet you all know what this room is, right?"

"The kitchen!" we all yelled.

"That's right. Now, what I bet you don't know is that the firefighters on duty have to go to the grocery store, buy all the food, and work as a team to cook the meals."

"Really?" said Chloe. "Don't you have a maid?"

"No, we don't," Captain Ken said, chuckling. "We have to do all the cooking and cleaning ourselves."

"Eewww," said Chloe, wrinkling up her nose. "That's a lot of work."

"Yes, it is. But it's fun, because we all work together. Would you like to see inside our food closet?"

"Yeah!"

Captain Ken opened up a huge closet next to the kitchen.

"Hey," said Max, "you guys eat a lot of the same stuff that I eat."

"Duh," Robbie whispered to me. "What does he think they are, aliens? Of course they eat the same food as us!"

"Is that candy?" Max asked, getting closer and closer to the closet.

"It sure is!"

"Why is that in there?"

"Do you like candy?" asked Captain Ken.

"Yeah, I love candy," said Max.

"No kidding," Jessie whispered. I giggled.

"Well," said Captain Ken, "we love candy, too. But we don't want to eat too much of it, because we have to stay in shape. Why don't you all follow me now, and I'll show you how we get our exercise."

We followed Captain Ken to a big room filled with gym equipment.

"This looks like the gym where my dad goes to work out," said Robbie.

"That's right," said Captain Ken. "Since we can't go to the gym when we are on duty, we set up a gym right here in the fire station."

"Cool."

"You have to be strong and healthy to fight fires, so we keep our muscles strong by working out with these machines. You have to have big muscles to slide down that fire pole."

I took one look at my teeny tiny muscles and moaned softly, "Ooooohhh nnnnoooooo."

"Follow me, everybody. We're going to go to our next room."

We followed Captain Ken down the hall to a big room filled with tables and chairs.

"Hey," said Max. "This looks like our classroom."

"That's exactly what it is," said Captain Ken.

"But the firefighters don't go to school," said Chloe.

"They don't go to school like you do, but every

time they are on duty, they come to this room to learn something new about fire safety or emergency rescue. We are going to come back to this room later in the tour, and I'm going to teach you some important things about fire safety. Because that is my number one job: making sure you all stay safe.

"Now come with me. I want to show you one last room before we go out to the garage to see the trucks.

"What do you think this room is?" asked Captain Ken.

"The TV room!" we all said together.

"That's right!"

"What kinds of shows do the firefighters like to watch?" asked Robbie.

"All different kinds of things," said Captain Ken. "Some guys like to watch baseball. Other guys like to watch wild animal shows."

"Hey, that's the same stuff I like to watch," said Robbie, laughing.

"What happens if you're watching TV and the alarm goes off? Does somebody turn off the TV?"

"That's a great question. If we are in the middle of doing something when the alarm sounds, then we have a master power switch that turns everything off when we leave. The TV, the oven, the lights."

"That's a good thing," said Jessie. "You wouldn't want to leave the stove on, or you might have a fire in the fire station!"

"Right!" Captain Ken said, chuckling. "We definitely would not want that! Come on, everybody. It's time to go out to the garage and see the trucks!"

We all cheered and followed Captain Ken out.

And my stomach did three more flips as we walked past the fire pole.

CHAPTER 6

Woo-oooo Woo-oooo Woo-oooo!

"First I am going to show you our firefighting uniform, and then I'll tell you about that big red engine over there. Follow me."

We walked across the garage to a row of cubbies. "Hey, those look like the cubbies that were in the bedroom upstairs," said Jessie.

"That's right," said Captain Ken. "The firefighters use the uniforms upstairs if they are woken up in the middle of the night, but if the alarm sounds during the day, then the firefighters just run into the garage and throw on their uniforms in here. What is your name, honey?"

"Jessie."

"Jessie, why don't you come over here, and I'll put the firefighter uniform on you?"

"That's not fair," Max whined.

"Maaaax," said Mrs. Wushy, giving him the angry stare. "Captain Ken chose Jessie. You need to be polite."

Captain Ken held up a piece of black fabric. "Does anyone know what this is?"

We all just stared at him.

"This is a special covering to protect your neck and ears." He put it over Jessie's head. "Then we put on these pants and this jacket." He slipped both of those on Jessie.

"The pants and the jacket are fire retardant, which means they can't catch on fire." He pulled open the jacket. "And look what's in here. It's a flashlight, in case it's very dark in the room we have to go into.

"Next we put on these boots." Jessie stepped into them. "Notice, boys and girls, that the boots have a hard part on the toe. Sometimes we might have to kick in a door, and this hard part protects our toes and feet from getting broken.

"How does all this stuff feel so far?"

"Heavy," Jessie said, laughing.

"Now let's add your helmet." He stuck the helmet on Jessie's head. It was a little big, so it fell over Jessie's face. Captain Ken knocked on the top of the helmet. "Hello? Anybody in there?"

"Yes," Jessie said, giggling.

He pushed the helmet up off Jessie's face. "The last thing we have to put on before we go into a burning building is this. Does anyone know what this is?"

"I do," said Robbie. "It's a gas mask. You have

to wear it so you can breathe the oxygen that is in a tube you carry on your back. Breathing the smoke from the fire is very dangerous."

Robbie is so smart. He knows everything about everything.

"You are absolutely right," said Captain Ken. "How did you know all that?"

"I read a lot," Robbie said, smiling.

"Good for you," said Captain Ken.

"Stay right there, Jessie," said Mrs. Wushy. "I want to get a picture of you in that uniform for our class scrapbook."

When Mrs. Wushy was done taking the picture, Jessie took off the uniform and we all walked over to the big red fire engine.

"Wow!" we said.

Just then we heard a bark, and a dalmatian jumped out of the fire truck.

"Well, look who's here!" said Captain Ken. "Boys and girls, I want you to meet Sparky. He lives here at the fire station."

"What was he doing in there?" I asked.

"Oh, that's his favorite place to sleep," said Captain Ken.

Sparky wagged his tail, barked, and ran off.

"Now, boys and girls," Captain Ken continued, "what do you need to put out a fire?"

"Water!"

"Right! Did you know that this truck can hold eight hundred gallons of water?"

"No way!"

"It has a huge water tank inside, and on the sides here are lots of hoses."

"Those hoses are really big," said Chloe. "I don't think I could pick one up."

"Well, you wouldn't have to," said Max. "Girls can't be firefighters."

"Oh yes they can," said Jessie. "I might be a firefighter when I grow up."

"That would be great!" said Captain Ken. "You know, we have two women who work at this fire station, and they are excellent firefighters. But everyone needs help with the hoses. At least two firefighters have to hold one hose, because the force of the water shooting

through the hose is really strong. It could actually knock you off your feet or send you flying into the air."

"Whoa!" said Robbie. "That force must be really strong."

"You have all been such good listeners.

Would you all like a chance to climb into the
fire truck?"

Before he finished his sentence, we had all
jumped onto the truck. "Hey, move out of the
way. I was here first," Max said, shoving Chloe
out of the front seat.

"No, you weren't. I was here first."

"No, I was, you little priss," he said, pushing her again.

"Mrs. Wushy," Chloe shouted, "Max pushed me."

Mrs. Wushy came over. "Max, come down off this truck right now."

"But . . ."

"No buts. You will have to wait a minute for your turn."

"But that's not fair."

"Oh, it's very fair. Now stand over here with me."

Robbie and I were sitting in the backseat of the fire truck, laughing and smiling and making siren noises. "Woo-oooo woo-oooo!"

I had almost forgotten about the fire pole when one of the firefighters came sliding down it right into the middle of the garage.

"Whoa. Did you see that?" asked Robbie.

"Yeah, I did."

"Come on over here, everybody. I want you to meet someone special. This is my son, Brad. He's a firefighter at this station, too. Brad, this is a first-grade class from Lincoln Elementary School."

"Welcome, everybody. Are you having fun with my dad?"

"Yes!" we all said.

I wasn't paying any attention to Brad. I just stood there staring up at the pole. It was really high. Even higher than I'd expected. I thought for a minute about hiding in one of the fire trucks until the tour was over, but before I could make a move, Robbie grabbed me by the arm and yanked me inside the fire station.

CHAPTER 7

Stop, Drop, and Roll

"Come on, Freddy," said Robbie. "We've got to hurry up. It's time for our fire safety lesson."

Captain Ken led everyone back to the classroom in the fire station. "Everybody, please find a seat. I am going to do a little lesson on fire safety now, and then I will choose a few lucky people to slide down the fire pole."

I closed my eyes and wished that this field trip was already over. When I opened my eyes, I was still sitting in the same place. "Why couldn't I have magic powers just this once?" I whispered to myself.

"Did you say something?" Captain Ken asked.

I realized he was talking to me. "Uh, no . . . nothing," I said.

"Okay, then let's get started. I'm going to ask you the most important question first. What should you do if you ever have an emergency?"

"Dial 911!" we all said together.

"Very good! If you ever have an emergency at your house—if your house is on fire, or somebody gets hurt—then you should call 911 right away. It's very important that you know your address, because the 911 operator will ask you what it is, so she knows where to send help. If you're not sure of your address, then go home tonight and practice it with your parents.

"Now, does anybody know what to do if your clothes catch on fire?"

Before anyone had a chance to answer, Max jumped out of his seat, dropped onto the floor,

and yelled, "Stop, drop, and roll! Stop, drop, and roll," demonstrating it as he said it.

"That is correct," said Captain Ken. "If your clothes catch on fire, then you should not run around. If you run around, the flames will get bigger. Instead, you should drop to the ground and roll around. That will put out the flames."

"Thank you for your answer, Max," said Mrs. Wushy, "but next time please wait to be called on."

Captain Ken continued. "Raise your hand if you have smoke detectors in your house."

Everybody's hands shot up.

"Excellent. That's what I like to see, because smoke detectors save lives. What should you do if your smoke detector goes off in the middle of the night?"

"Get out of the house," said Jessie.

"Exactly," said Captain Ken. "How many ways are there to get out of your room?"

"Oh, I know this one," said Chloe. "One way. Out through your bedroom door."

"Actually," said Captain Ken, "there is a second way out. Does anyone know what it is?"

Robbie raised his hand. "I know. You could go out the window."

"Very good, Robbie," said Captain Ken. "That is correct. If you smell smoke in your house, crawl to your bedroom door and feel the door with the back of your hand. If your door feels hot, then don't open it. Climb out the window instead or, if your bedroom is not on the ground floor, then open the window and wait for the firefighters to arrive."

"Why do I have to crawl?" asked Chloe.

"Because if your house is filling up with smoke, you don't want to breathe in that smoke. It's not good for you. The cleaner air is closer to the ground, so that is why you should crawl. Once you are outside, should you go back in to get your teddy bear or your special blanket?"

"If I left my china doll in my room, then I would have to go back and get it. It is a special present from my nana. She had it when she was a little girl," said Chloe. "If it got burned, I would never be able to get another one. They don't make them anymore."

"Well, my *abuela*, my grandma, always tells me that I should never go back in," said Jessie. "She says that she can buy another bear or another toy, but she can't buy another me."

"That's right. Your grandma is a very smart lady. You should never go back inside a burning building. I know the doll your nana gave you is one of a kind, Chloe, but no toy is more important than your life. I know your grandma would never want to lose you."

"No, she wouldn't," said Chloe. "She always tells me how precious I am."

"I think I'm going to be sick," whispered Jessie.

Robbie giggled.

"Okay, moving on," Captain Ken continued. "How many of you have a family meeting place for once you get outside?"

"I do," said Robbie. "If there ever is a fire in the house, then my sister and I are supposed to get out as quickly as possible and then meet my parents at the big tree in the front yard."

"That's a great meeting spot. Does anyone else have one?"

"I'm supposed to go to my neighbor's house," said Max.

"That's another good idea. You all are so smart," said Captain Ken. "Now that we all know how important smoke detectors are, you should check them often to make sure they are working."

"I always know when the battery is getting low," said Jessie, "because it starts chirping like a bird."

"Yes, that's one way to know that it needs a new battery, but it's better not to wait that long," said Captain Ken. "I think it's a good idea to check them once a month. You could remind your parents at the beginning of each month to check the smoke detectors. It only takes a few minutes, and it saves lives.

"Let's just talk about a few more things, and then we'll do the fire pole."

Time was running out. I had to think of something fast. I raised my hand.

"Yes?" said Captain Ken.

"May I please go to the bathroom?"

"Of course you can. There is one right down the hall. Would you like me to have Brad show you where it is?"

"Uh, no. That's okay," I said. "I can find it myself." The truth was, I wasn't really going to

go to the bathroom. I was going to find a place to hide until our visit was over. There was no way I would ever have the guts to slide down that pole, and I didn't want Max calling me a baby for the rest of my life. If I just disappeared for a little bit, no one would know that I was gone. I would just reappear when the pole-sliding part was over and act like I was sorry I'd missed it.

I tiptoed out of the room as Captain Ken was

reminding everyone never to pull the fire alarm at school as a joke. I quietly walked down the hall and into the garage. I decided that one of the fire trucks would be the best place to hide. I walked over to the shiny big red fire engine that Robbie and I had been playing in earlier and climbed up. Sparky was sleeping on the seat. He jumped up when I stepped inside.

"Hey, boy," I whispered. I patted his head so he wouldn't start barking. Then I got down on the floor so nobody would be able to see me in there, and I lay perfectly still without making a sound. Sparky curled up next to me. The only things I could hear were the sound of his breathing and the beating of my heart . . . *thump . . . thump . . . thump.*

CHAPTER 8

Emergency!

"Emergency! Emergency!" I heard the voice calling.

Oh no! I thought. *What happened? Is somebody hurt?*

The voice got closer and closer and louder and louder, and then I realized it was Mrs. Wushy. "Help me, please. Somebody help me, please!"

"Mrs. Wushy, what is the problem?" I heard Captain Ken say.

"You know how one of my students asked to go to the bathroom?"

"Yes."

"Well, he didn't come back, so I went to look in the bathroom, and he wasn't there. I don't know where he is. I'm really worried that something happened to him."

"Don't worry, Mrs. Wushy. I'm sure he's all right. Brad will stay with the rest of the class while I help you find him."

"I sure hope he's okay!"

Wow! I'd had no idea that my hiding was going to be such a problem. I had never thought that Mrs. Wushy would even notice.

"Freddy! Freddy!" she called. "Where are you?"

Just then I felt a hand on my leg, and I screamed, "AAAAHHH!"

Sparky barked.

"It's okay, Freddy. It's just me," said Captain

Ken, and he lifted me out of the truck. "Mrs. Wushy, I think I found your missing student."

Mrs. Wushy ran over. "Oh my goodness, Freddy. Are you all right? What were you doing out here?"

I started to cry. "I . . . I . . . I'm so sorry . . . Mrs. Wushy. . . . I didn't . . . mean . . . to . . . scare . . . you . . . ," I said between sobs.

"But why are you hiding?"

"If I tell you, then you won't laugh at me?"

"Of course not, Freddy."

"I was afraid to slide down the fire pole, but if I didn't do it, then everyone would think I was a baby and a fraidy-cat."

"Freddy, do you want me to let you in on a little secret?" said Captain Ken.

"Sure."

"Just because you get scared sometimes doesn't mean you're a fraidy-cat."

"But *you* never get scared."

"You wanna bet? There are plenty of times I see a huge fire and get really scared to run into the burning building."

"Really?"

"Yes, really. Does that mean I'm a baby?"

"No, you're really brave!"

"Well, thank you very much. You know, you can be brave, too."

"I can?"

"Yep. Whenever you get scared, just tell yourself to be brave. Take a few deep breaths and go for it."

"I guess I could try that."

"Well then, how about trying that right now?"

"Now?"

"Yep. We'll go get the rest of the class, and you can be the first one down the pole."

I swallowed hard and looked up at the pole.

"Come on. You can do it. I know you can," said Captain Ken. "Don't let your fear stop you from trying things. And I'll be waiting at the bottom to catch you."

Captain Ken took my hand, and we went to get the rest of the class.

"Freddy, Freddy, are you all right?" asked Jessie and Robbie.

Captain Ken winked at me. "He's better than all right. He's great. He just took a wrong turn coming back from the bathroom. Come on, everybody. It's time for the fire pole, and Freddy is going to go first."

Robbie stared at me and mouthed, *Are you crazy?*

I just shook my head and mouthed, *Come on!*

We all went upstairs to the top of the fire pole. "I'm going to slide down first so I can catch you at the bottom, and then Freddy is going to go next. Ready?"

"Freddy?" said Max. "He's even afraid to go on the monkey bars at school. He's never going to go down that pole."

"Max," said Mrs. Wushy, "that is not very nice."

"Oh, I think you'll be surprised at how brave Freddy is," said Captain Ken. "Just you watch."

He jumped onto the pole and slid down. He made it look so easy.

"Okay, Freddy, now it's your turn. Remember, picture yourself sliding down the pole and landing safely on the ground. You can do it!"

I took a deep breath. *You can do it. You can do it,* I said to myself. Then, before I could change my mind, I jumped and grabbed the pole.

I slid down so fast that the whole ride seemed like it lasted two seconds. Captain Ken caught me at the bottom.

Sparky barked and jumped up to lick my face.

I could hear all my classmates cheering for me at the top. "Woohoo! All right, Freddy. You did it! You were awesome!"

Captain Ken squeezed my hand and smiled. "See, what did I tell you? I knew you could do it. Even fraidy-cats can be brave."

"Was it scary?" Jessie yelled down from the top of the pole.

"Nah. It was actually really fun. I want to do it again," I said.

Captain Ken laughed. "Maybe you'll be a firefighter someday. We need brave people like you."

"Maybe I will," I said, and smiled a great big smile. "Maybe I will."

DEAR READER,

I am a kindergarten and first-grade teacher, and every year in October, the firefighters from our town come to talk to my students about fire safety. The firefighters always teach my students some fire safety tips that I have included in the back of this book.

I think one of the most important things that the firefighters teach us is that if there is a fire, you get out and stay out. You should NEVER go back into a burning building to get something you left inside. Your mom and dad can always get you another teddy bear, but they cannot get another you!

I remember the night my neighbor's house caught on fire. It was very scary. But the first thing my family did was make sure that they had all gotten out of the house all right. We were so glad that they had all made it out safely. That is why it is important to make an escape plan with your family, so you all know how to get safely out of your house in case of a fire.

I'm sure you know some other good fire safety tips that I did not include in the book. I would love to hear about them. Just write to me at:

Ready, Freddy! Fun Stuff

c/o Scholastic Inc.

P.O. Box 711

New York, NY 10013-0711

I hope you had as much fun reading *Firehouse Fun!* as I had writing it!

HAPPY READING!

Abby Klein

Freddy's Fun Pages

FREDDY'S SHARK JOURNAL

HOW CAN YOU AVOID A SHARK ATTACK?

Follow these rules:

Don't swim in water that you know may have sharks.

Do not go into the water if you are bleeding from a cut or a scrape. Sharks are attracted to the smell of blood.

Always swim with a buddy.

Swim in clear water. If the water is murky, a shark might mistake you for a sea creature it likes to eat.

If someone sees a shark, try to get out of the water quickly without splashing too much.

FREDDY AND CAPTAIN KEN'S FIRE SAFETY TIPS

1. If you see a fire, call 911 right away.

2. If your clothes catch on fire, stop, drop, and roll.

3. Regularly check all the smoke detectors in your house and replace the batteries when needed.

4. If there is a fire in your house, feel your bedroom door with the back of your hand. If the door feels hot, do not open the door. Find another way out.

5. Make sure you know two ways out of your house. Draw an escape map with your family, so you know how to get out of your house in case of a fire.

🔥 6. If a building is full of smoke, and you are trying to get out, crawl along the ground, so you don't breathe in too much smoke.

🔥 7. Get out of a burning building as quickly as possible and stay out. Do not go back inside for any reason.

🔥 8. Set up a family meeting place somewhere outside your house where you will all go once you get out of the burning building.

🔥 9. Never play with matches.

Every family should have a fire escape plan. You can draw one on the following page. Follow these simple steps:

1. Draw and label the floor plan of your house.

2. Draw arrows showing escape routes to at least two exits (windows or outside doors). Be sure to make the routes as short as possible.

3. Walk through the escape routes with your family so you are familiar with them.

4. Practice fire drills several times a year.

HOME FIRE ESCAPE PLAN

Draw the rooms of your house so you know
which way to turn in the event of a fire.

FIRE SAFETY WORD GAME

How many different words can you
make from the words:

FIRE SAFETY

_____

_____

_____

_____

_____

_____

_____

COUNT THE SPOTS

How many spots can you find
on this dalmatian?

Have you read all about Freddy?

Don't miss any of Freddy's
funny adventures!